The Adventures Lilly Nilly

Pardon My French

It's the Language of Ballet

Written & Illustrated by Nancy Paris

Dedicated to my sister Robin Paris for her total awesomeness,
to Lady Colleen Heller who always encourages me to reach farther,
to Jaye Medalia for her guidance and artistic eye, and to my
husband Charles Yurick, who thought it was a good idea to marry
a grown-up Lilly Nilly.

ISBN: 978-0-578-31688-8

Book design by Jaye Medalia

www.lillynilly.com

Blue is for Babies

Now, here's something you should know. My name is Lilly. My mom calls me Lilly Nilly when she's mad. That's my whole name, but don't you call me that. Because, by the time you get it out, I'll be long gone.

Ask my mom. When I was little, I was supercute. But when I hit six, things went south. I'm way too tall, my bangs are way too short, and my ballet bun looks like a big red eraser on the top of my head.

My Aunt Lillian calls me "Lencil the Pencil." My dad calls me "Ticonderoga #2."

Sometimes being a ballerina can be boring. I should know because I've been one almost my entire life. And, as you know, I'm already six.

Well, not always boring. Like the time when I was five and a girl peed on the floor before our teacher Miss Katie started ballet class. So, when Miss Katie ran to get a mop, it was MY idea to jump over the puddle, just like we do when we practice our leaps in class.

Only this time, there was a real puddle, and we left our footprints all over the floor. None of us got a lollipop that day.

Did you know you can't wear a sparkly dress in ballet class? I saw *The Nutcracker* once, and that's why I even wanted to be a ballerina in the first place. But in my ballet school, the rules say you have to wear a baby blue leotard when you are five and a pink leotard when you are six. Boring!

Once, I asked Miss Katie if I could wear a princess crown with my leotard. She said I had to wait until Halloween.

Miss Katie can wear whatever she wants when she teaches Blue ballet—supercute lime green leggings, or purple dance sneakers, or anything, so long as it's fashion forward.

Miss Katie's mom is Miss Susan, the boss of my whole ballet school. Miss Susan used to be kind of wrinkly, but not since she got those shots that freeze your face. In Show and Tell at school, we talk about special or unique things. So, I decided to scotch tape my whole face to show the class what Miss Susan's frozen face looks like. I wanted to tell them what it feels like too, but I couldn't because I accidently taped my mouth shut. I must rethink these scientific investigations.

The other thing I forgot to tell you is that Miss Katie can't wear her nose ring when she teaches anymore. Because it got stuck on a kid's hair bow, and it was pretty nasty. It looked like a pile-up on the Long Island Expressway.
It took two moms to unhook them.

I really wanted red ballet slippers, but nobody ever listens to me. They gave me pink instead. My mom made sure I got them extra big so I wouldn't grow out of them so fast. People, it's not my fault if I hop across the room, but one of my shoes doesn't finish the trip. By the way, ballet slippers don't look like slippers at all.

Last year, when I was in the baby Blue class, I wanted to do real ballet. Turns! Splits! And those things they call Beeps! You know, when you bonk your legs together? But nooo! Instead, we had to do things like bend our knees to make diamond shapes with our legs, count to eight in French, or march around the room. Yes, that's what we did. Every. Single. Class. That, and jump over puddles. But you already know that.

One day, Miss Katie said that we were going to learn a special dance for the Spring recital. At last! Real ballet in sparkly dresses and princess crowns!

Miss Katie was very excited. She said we would be dancing to "Twinkle Twinkle Little Star." I was hoping for Stravinsky.

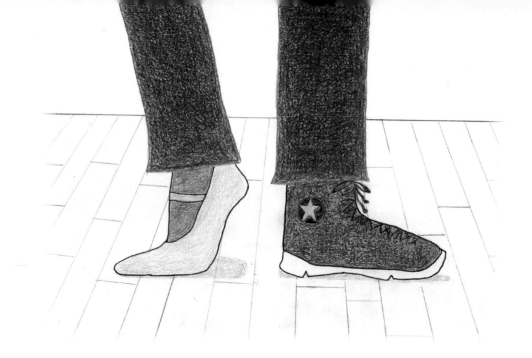

Mr. Paul in Pink

Now that I'm in Pink ballet (remember I'm six), we get a new teacher. His name is Mr. Paul, and he doesn't look like a ballet teacher at all, except that he knows French words and the place where the real ballet teachers hide the lollipops.

Mr. Paul wears one sneaker and one ballet shoe. No one knows for sure why. He told us that he used to dance on cruise ships. I don't know, is that a thing?

Sometimes life doesn't turn out the way you think. Like when I thought I'd be able to run faster and jump higher wearing my new Keds. At least that's what they said on TV. But, trust me, that's not what happened when I tried to climb the refrigerator case at the supermarket.

Back to ballet...

At first, I was sure I would never like the baby Blue class, and I never did get to dance to Stravinsky. But I did get to dance all by myself. It's called a solo, and I was Tinkerbell! I finally got to wear a sparkly Tinkerbell dress. Oh, excuse me—*tutu*. I must use my French.

I'll bet you think I speak French a lot by now, but I really don't. The only French we learned in Blue ballet was counting to eight and "inky dinky parlez-vous." Oh wait, that last thing I learned in day camp.

Anyway, at my recital, two things happened in my tutu. The first thing was that Miss Katie had to push me out on stage because I couldn't hear the music with all those big stage curtains in the way. The second thing was that the audience clapped way before I finished my dance. So, I gave them a dirty look, and they stopped.

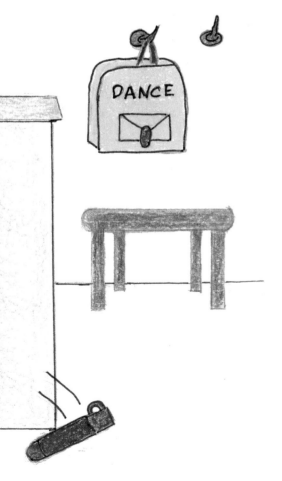

Then, at the REAL end, I did my bow, and everyone clapped like they're supposed to. Then I got fried clams and ice cream. I will remember that day for the rest of my life, or at least until high school.

Anyway, all the teachers at my school have to wear shirts with the name of our school written on the front: Dance Utopia of Massapequa. I will never wear one of those shirts in a million years. Because the initials spell D.U.M. When Mr. Paul wears his shirt tied around his waist, it says D.U.M on his B.U.M.

You might ask if ballerinos like Mr. Paul wear ballet buns. Apparently not, and it's a good thing because Mr. Paul's hair looks like Miss Katie's cockapoo. He would need like a zillion hair pins to get it up.

In Pink ballet we get to stand at a wooden bar called a *barre* (duh). Last year, we didn't do that. Last year, I used to hang upside down on the *barre* because I thought it was just a "bar."

Miss Katie always asked me, "Are you a ballerina or a monkey?" I guess ballerinas don't like to look like monkeys.

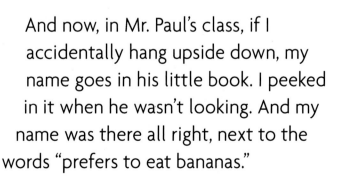

And now, in Mr. Paul's class, if I accidentally hang upside down, my name goes in his little book. I peeked in it when he wasn't looking. And my name was there all right, next to the words "prefers to eat bananas."

Remember I told you that last year some things were boring?
Like when we had to stand in the middle of the room and bend
our knees to make a diamond shape with our legs?

I didn't tell you the really hard part—we had to do it while our heels were kissing and our feet made the letter "V." You try it.

But this year I found out that making diamond shapes with your legs is really ballet because it has a French name. It's called *demi plié*. I think it means HALF a *plié* because you're a baby, but I can't be sure.

Now we do the hard version called *grand plié*. You go down way past *demi plié*, like an elevator going to the basement, and then you come up again to the main floor. Mr. Paul showed us once and we had to copy him. But I was the only kid that went down and up like an elevator at Macy's. Still, I kind of wished that I was home watching TV instead of pretending to be an elevator.

Then Mr. Paul asked me to show my *grand plié* to the class.

Uh-oh, did I do it all wrong? Should I do it again, but different? So, I decided I will do it again just the same way. If it's wrong, I wouldn't mind being home on Wednesday afternoons.

I stood at the *barre* and made sure my heels were kissing and my feet looked like a "V." I made my trip down and up. What can I tell you? Mr. Paul said I did it perfectly and everyone should do it again just like me. I felt so proud, and that's when I knew...

DANCING IS AWESOME!

Bras for Arms

I just found out something today. I'm not a ballerina, I'm a BALLET DANCER. You can't be a ballerina until you're old, like 26. Mr. Paul said a ballerina has to work very hard for years and years to be better than everyone else, and then you have to dance for the President of the United States. (I just made that last part up, but you get where I'm going with this.)

I'm learning a lot of new things these days. Like the way my mom told me how I would get to dance class. It's called a "carpool." That sounded like fun, so I thought I should wear a bathing suit instead of my leotard.

It was a simple question, but my mom laughed, and the coffee she was drinking squirted out of her nose, right onto the kitchen table. I swear I saw some boogers floating in it, too. Gross.

The other gross thing I recently learned was the word "wedgie." It's happened to me before, but who knew it had a name? When you wear a leotard, it's easy to get one. Especially when you bend all the way forward and come back up.

When I got my first ballet wedgie, I tried to wiggle it out on the way down. That didn't work, so I just pulled it out on the way up. Mr. Paul said not to do that. He said, "What would you do if it happened on stage?"

He has a point, so now I wait until the exercise is over before I unwedge.

Mr. Paul also said that the way you move your arms is called *port de bras.* BRA! When we all stopped laughing, Mr. Paul said that *bras* means "arms" in French. Then what do French moms wear under their shirts? ARMS??

Which reminds me, Rhonda Malfara, one of the kids in my ballet class, wears her bathing suit top under her undershirt and calls it a bra. Her bathing suit top has creepy little clown faces all over it, so she does not look grown up at all! But try telling Rhonda that.

She thinks she's so great because she has supercute bangs and curly brown hair all the way down to her butt. Everyone always says that she looks like a princess, and maybe she does. But if she ever shows up to ballet wearing a princess crown, I will personally remove it.

And it's not just her princess hair that makes me go all Crabby McStabby. She calls me "Super Silly Lilly Nilly." I should call her "stupid," but I know that only sisters are allowed to call each other "stupid."

Anyway, I got kind of mad at my mom. Didn't she know about rhymes back when she was picking out names? My sister Robin was named after a bird. Why couldn't I be named after a different flower? I asked my mom to change my name to Daisy. That sounded pretty safe. She said Daisy rhymes with "crazy" and "lazy." I guess you can't win. Someone will always find a dumb name that rhymes with yours.

And I found one for Rhonda. It's Shanda. Rhonda Shanda, Rhonda Shanda. If you have a Jewish grandma, ask her what "shanda" means. If you don't have one, I'll tell you myself. It means "shame on you for calling me names."

Sometimes little kids say mean things, and sometimes other kids laugh at you. But now that I'm six, I know it doesn't matter. Because when I grow up, I'm going to be a dancer. Maybe even a ballerina. And Rhonda? She'll probably be a dentist.

Inchworms in America

Miss Agnes is the lady that plays the piano for Pink Ballet. I heard that she was a famous ballerina a million years ago, and that the flowered chiffon skirt she wears is from around the time that ballet was invented. But nowadays at Dance Utopia, she only does hip-hop.

Miss Agnes was watching us today when Mr. Paul taught us how to sashay. No, wait—*chassé*. Whatever. The step goes sideways, and it's really slow. When we do it I think we all look like pink inchworms. I told Miss Agnes that she should play the song "Inchworm" to get us in the mood. She made her eyes real squinty and told me she doesn't take requests.

Anyway, there we were, inchworming across the floor as Miss Agnes banged out "The Battle Hymn of the Republic." Mr. Paul made us inch-worm back and forth across the floor. Back and forth and back and forth about 14 times in a row until I was sick of it. Mr. Paul says that we have to practice it A LOT because we're going to do it for our parents in the Spring recital.

Do you think our parents will want to watch us do ANYTHING 14 times in a row? I can tell you from experience. They won't.

Here's my point. We have to do these sashays with our hands on our waist, like the sugar bowl in my Beauty and the Beast tea set. Mr. Paul said that it's a hard step for kids, so first we have to learn what the feet do, and later we will learn a nice way to move our *bras*. (I'm using the French word here, so don't freak out.) But, people, seriously—what's so hard about moving your *bras* and legs at the same time? I've been doing that for years. And if I've been doing it all wrong, well, nobody ever mentioned it. PLUS, Mr. Paul kept yelling that we should not look BORED when we do it. We have to think of a way to make it look interesting and supercute so that our parents will let us come back to ballet next year. I thought, "Good luck with that."

And then it hit me! Mr. Paul has a surprise for us! Pretend that it's the Spring recital, and even though I probably won't ever invite you, you're in the audience watching me dance. Everyone in my Pink class isn't just inching across the stage doing the same wormy step with our hands stuck on our waist—we're doing a special BEAUTY AND THE BEAST DANCE! We're the sugar bowls, and the older kids are plates and forks! (Please note: The babies aren't in this. All they get is "Twinkle Twinkle Little Star." As my dad says, "You have to pay your dues.")

I think I'm right about this. I think. I'll have to give it more thought. There is one thing I do know for sure, and it's because of my science class in school. No matter what I do, my sashay will never be as interesting as the inside of a whale's mouth.

Sugar Plum Sherry

Having a fight with my ballet buddy at my dance recital wasn't the best idea, especially since it happened in the middle of Sugar Plum Fairy.

I guess Mr. Paul was nervous that we would all forget the dance, so during the show he hid behind the curtain and called out the steps.

We were the only ones who could hear him, not our parents. I thought it was a supercool way to make our parents think that we were really smart and remembered everything. We didn't.

We were good until right after the tap, tap, 1-2-3!! Tap, tap, 1-2-3!! After that, the music tinkles. We each had to listen for our own personal tinkle and then grab our buddy's hand and run to the front of the stage. Then you're supposed to stand on your knees way too long and wait for everyone's tinkles to stop.

Only my friend Sherry didn't do that. All she wanted to do was stand there with big blobby tears pouring out of her blobby brown eyes and messing up her stage make-up.

She was stuck like a statue in the back while everyone else was Sugar Plumming in the front. It was like someone had glued her feet to the floor. She did not move.

I kept pulling and pulling on her to come with me, and Mr. Paul kept shouting, "Run! Run!" So, I ran. Without Sherry. I left my friend.

In regular school, we learned about consequences. And that's kind of what happened next. I got to the front of the stage just as everyone's tinkles stopped. In the next part of the dance you form a circle with your *bras* and lift them up so that it looks like a pretend picture frame for your head. It's simple if you don't have a big head. Or short arms.

I was so happy to be back dancing in the front, I threw my two *bras* up in the air and made the picture frame around my head, just like Mr. Paul said. And that's when it happened. Both shoulder straps on my costume busted at the same time. The top of my costume rolled down past my nickels and onto my waist where it got all bunchy. I guess my mom hadn't sewn the straps on tight enough. My white top looked like an innertube floaty on my pretty red *tutu*.

Maybe I cried. I don't remember. It's possible.

I learned two really important things at my recital that day: never leave your friend if she is crying, and never let my mom anywhere near your costume.

Butt Heads

You'll never guess what! We have a substitute ballet teacher for the last few weeks before summer vacation. Miss Susan, the blond lady who owns D.U.M. and a motorcycle, said that Mr. Paul was taking some personal time off.

My mom said it's because we were driving Mr. Paul bonkers during our recital. But what I think really happened is that Miss Susan gave Mr. Paul a personal time out because of another word he taught us last week—*DERRIÈRE!* You just don't say that around kids if you're not their dad.

At my house, my mom says "*derrière*." She also says "the part that went over the fence post last." I don't know, maybe she grew up with chickens.

Did you ever stop to think why there are so many names for your butt? There's your "behind," or "tushy," or "booty"—or another word that I got a time out for saying. I'll leave it at that.

My new substitute teacher is Miss Ella, and she's from France! Mr. Paul is from New Jersey, which explains a lot.

My mom called Miss Ella a "skinnymalink," so I asked her what that means. She said it's Irish for "really pretty." My mom likes to speak Irish a lot. Her favorite thing to say is "jesus-son-of-mary-and-joseph."

À LA SECONDE

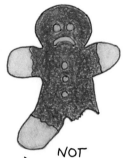

NOT
À LA SECONDE

MY SISTER

EATING À LA SECONDE

Then my mom said that because Miss Ella is from France, Miss Susan has to pay her under the table. I'm a little low on my allowance, so I watched them when they sat down to eat their lunch. Just in case they dropped some change. Cha-ching! Nope. Nothing. Nada.

Ha-ha, people, very funny. Don't you think I know that my mom was only joking? Lilly Nilly wasn't born yesterday! Miss Ella gets paid like everyone else—from the ATM.

Miss Ella calls our butt *le popo*. That's supercute and avoids confusion. Today she said that *derrière* means anything that happens in back of you, I'm guessing by your butt. *À la seconde* means that you stand there with your leg stuck out to the side like a gingerbread man before your sister gets hold of it.

But what is the French word for your front parts? I don't even know exactly what the English word is. I'm sure it's not the word that we use at home. Maybe this is something we should discuss.

Boy, do I have a zillion questions to ask Miss Ella!
Like, what DO French moms wear under their
shirts? And do French kids in ballet school have
to learn their positions in English? In ballet class
do they say "front, side, and badonkadonk?"
I really don't think so, but I want to see
the look on Miss Ella's face
when I ask her. Anyway, I
will learn some more ballet words
and report back.

I saw a movie about a famous ballerino. He was
from someplace like Russia, or maybe Canada.
I got to thinking, where are all the boys in my
ballet school?

I don't like boys, but when I'm older, I definitely
want to be lifted high in the air by one. And
that's not something you go to college to
learn. Except my friend Nicole's older
brother said he wants to go to college
to pick up girls. So... maybe you do.
I'm going to ask Miss Ella.

Not So D.U.M.

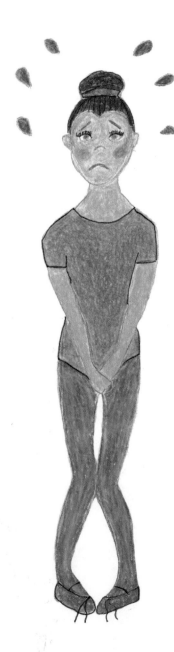

Now that I look back at my Blue and Pink ballet years, I guess I have learned a few things, which I have outlined below:

★ You better pee before you start your ballet class.

★ Trust yourself a little bit more because you might be right. And if you're not, and you mess up a little, well, elevators weren't built in a day.

★ It's not a good idea to do something bad to someone just because they did something bad to you. Because Rhonda is now my best friend, and I want to barf anytime I hear a grandma shout, "It's a Shanda!"

★ If you have a problem like a ballet wedgie, get to the bottom of it (LOL!). Ask an older kid. I did, and I learned something they don't teach you in ballet class. It turns out that you're not supposed to wear underwear under your tights.

I guess I won't be sharing my leotard with my sister.

⭐ Don't trust your parents to tell you the real name of your body parts. Ask a friend.

⭐ If someone makes you practice a thing 14 times in a row so that you can do it better, you might as well do it instead of just pretending. And it's not only in ballet. Because when my mom told me to brush my teeth, I just sat in the bathroom for ten minutes holding my toothbrush. Now I have a cavity.

Here's my poem on the subject:
Put in the time
To get rid of the slime.
You can't fool
   Mother Nature.

⭐ And, people, don't give up on your friends when they get scared, especially if their mom is good with a needle and thread.

⭐ But, most of all, don't laugh at the French. They invented mayonnaise.

Made in the USA
Middletown, DE
12 January 2022